For Suzanne

First published 2013 by Macmillan Children's Books
a division of Macmillan Publishers Limited
20 New Wharf Road, London N1 9RR
Basingstoke and Oxford
Associated companies throughout the world
www.panmacmillan.com
www.emilygravett.com

ISBN: 978-0-230-74538-4

1 3 5 7 9 8 6 4 2

A CIP catalogue record for this book is available from the British Library.

Printed in China

This book belongs to:

....

& Little Mouse

Little Mouse's

Emily Gravett's

Big
Book
of
Beasts

Macmillan Children's Books

LION

The lion is a mighty king.
He's sharp of tooth
And sharp of claw,
Fleet of foot
And loud of . . .

I do NOT
like
LOUD
lions,

SHHHHH

PRETTY MITTENS

Eeeek!
How to make this page less scary
1) Remove roar
2) Cover claws
3) Turn the page
ROAR!
100% CAT HAIR

ORIGAMICE

Projects for the nimble pawed

Or sharp-tempered sharks.

SHARK

The Great White Shark
Has many teeth,
Too numerous to count.
(Unless you're very, very close
And then it's paramount.)

BEAR

The bear can be grizzly, brown, black or white,
And when angered he makes a formidable sight.
He can survive in forests, up mountains, on snow,
There are very few places a bear CANNOT go!

I think bears are UN-BEARABLE,

ESCAPE YOUR WORRIES IN ONE BOUNCE

Bounce high from our biggest chair.
Note how the luxury bear hair
stuffing on silent tensioned spri
allows maximum lift-off.

Send coupon today for
details of our Spring O

ONE BOUNCE CHAIRS LTD

Please send me straight to the next page because this bear is scar

NAME ... Little Mouse

ADDRESS ... The bookshelf

WASP

The first you hear
When wasps are near
Is a buzzing in your ear.
The second thing
Is when they sting.
OUCH!

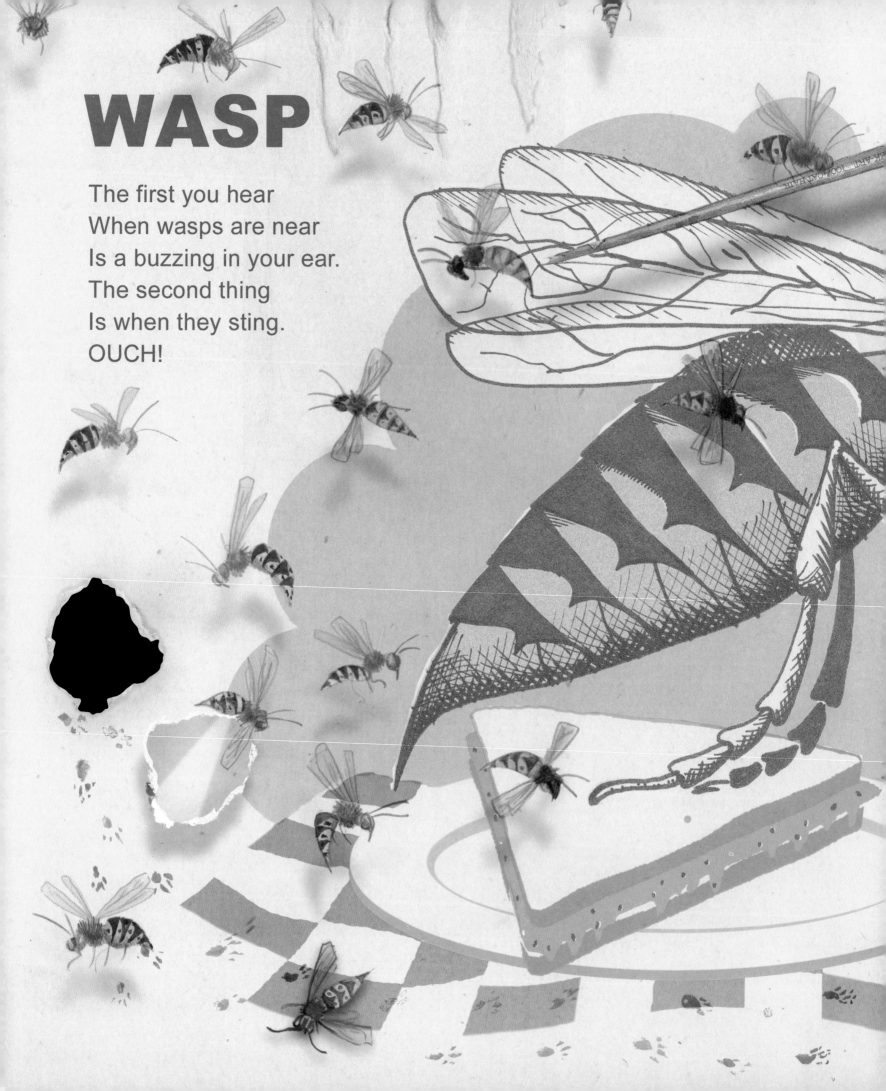

Wasps worry me,

And crabs give

me the creeps.

CRAB

This crab . . .
Was made to grab.

CROCODILE

Never ever be beguiled
By a smiling crocodile.
He isn't friendly in the least,
In fact he's quite a nasty beast.

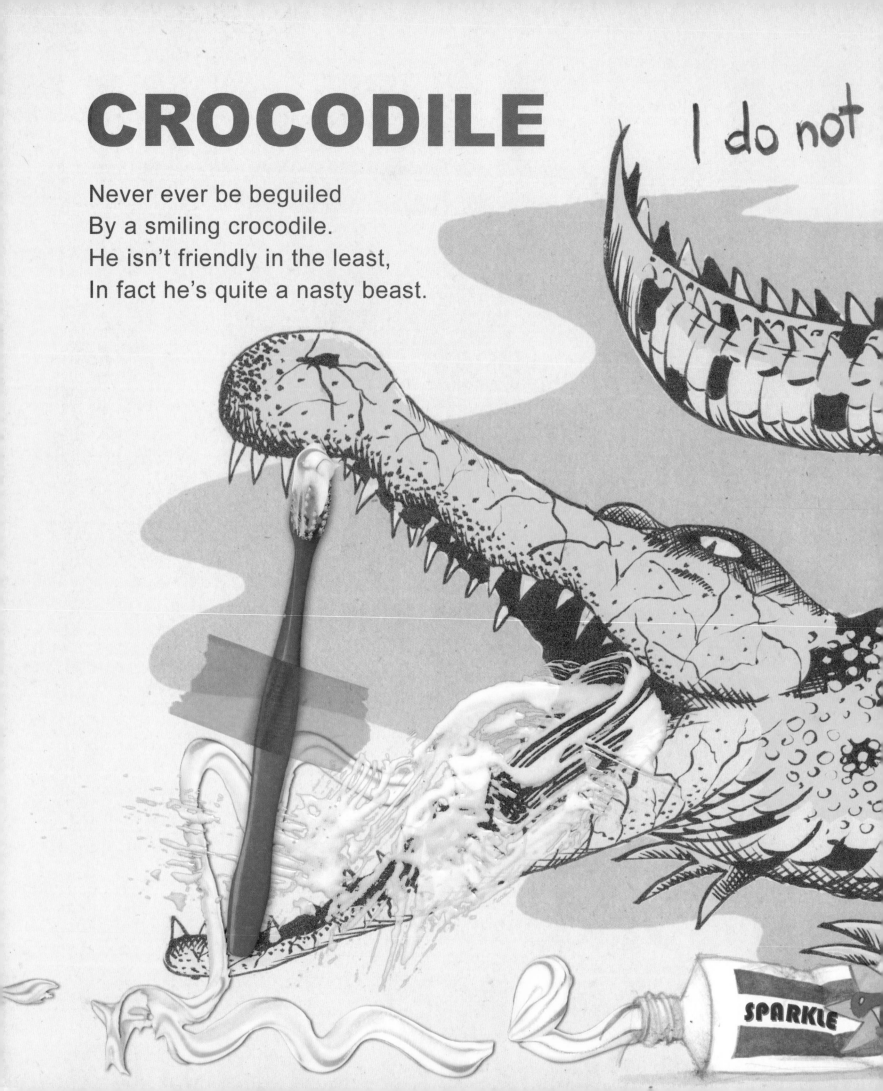

want to be crunched by a crocodile,

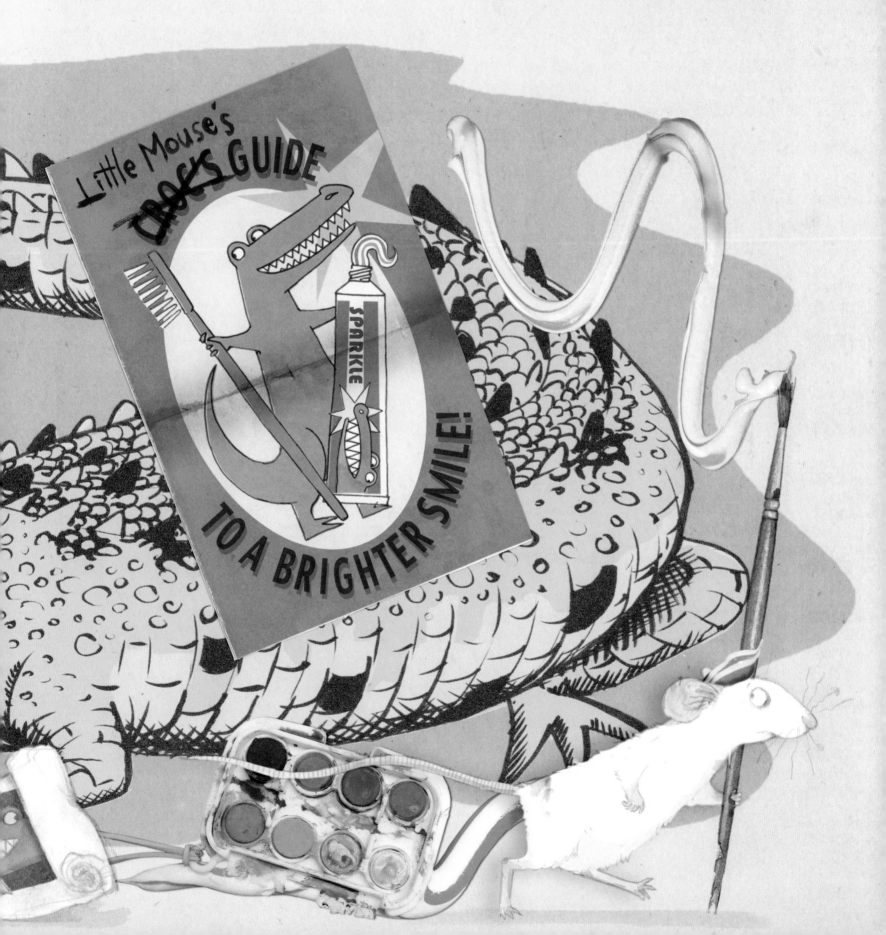

RHINOCEROS

The rhino cannot be accused
Of daintiness and grace.
And when stampeding, you should know,
It builds up quite a pace.

Run down by a rhino,

Dainty Shoes

Elegance
At
Your
Feet

OWL

The owl by day
Is fast asleep,
Dreaming of his lunch.

By night, in flight,
He hunts for mice,
Then eats them with a
CRUNCH!

JELLYFISH

A jellyfish
Is not a dish.
But is in fact
A sort of fish
(Which stings.)

I prefer jelly dishes to jelly fishes,

SNAKE

Some snakes kill with poison,
But the Boa-Constrictor
Seizes
Then squeeeeezes,
Then swallows 'em whole.

MOUSE!

MAKE YOUR OWN BEAST

Stick body here

You will need
Heads, Body, Legs, Ears, Mouth,
and anything else you want!